Secrets of the Toad

Trisha

Secrets of the Toad

Reflection

By Trisha

gatekeeper press
Columbus, Ohio

Cover Illustration – Lydia Zwierzynski – http://www.lydiagraphics.com
Interior Illustrations – Beth Parrish

Secrets of the Toad: Reflection

Published by Gatekeeper Press
2167 Stringtown Rd, Suite 109
Columbus, OH 43123-2989
www.GatekeeperPress.com

The cover design, interior formatting, typesetting, and editorial work for this book are entirely the product of the author. Gatekeeper Press did not participate in and is not responsible for any aspect of these elements.

(paperback): 9781642378870
eISBN: 9781642378887

Contents

Chapter **1**

Bus Ride Home

Emma is just sooo glad that this school day is over! There is just no way that it could have been any worse. She leans her head into the back of the brown vinyl seat in front of her. It feels cool, and through it, she can feel her bumpy ride home.

Here she sits alone two seats behind her bus driver, Mr. Norris. You know, in one of those seats that are usually assigned for the troublemakers or chosen by one of the nerdy kids. But Mr. Norris doesn't assign seats. Emma sits here as an outcast after being ignored by her best friend, Chloe, all day long. No, make that all week long. She has been ignored not just by Chloe but by all of her so-called friends. Emma twirls a strand of hair around her pointer finger as she eavesdrops on the conversations behind her.

Hmm, it sounds like Chloe and Mary Rose might be making plans for the weekend. What are they going to do? Emma steals a quick glance behind her while not wanting to be seen. It looks like the whole entire bus is having a grand old time. Everyone is smiling and laughing. And there is her older brother, Jacob Andrew Wright, or Jake for short. He is surrounded by a bunch of friends. If I ask, maybe he'll clue me in to how he does it. Or maybe it's just because he's so cute – dirty blond hair and blue eyes. He's got that dimple – Dad's dimple. Lucky him. Wish I could look like Jake. Heck, it even looks like the girls are flirting with him.

Emma has seen enough. She retreats and returns her head to the seat in front of her.

Sure sounds like they're having a fun time back there. A great friend you are, Chloe. I wish I could be cool and popular like Jake.

Whispers. Was that my name I heard? Emma strains her ears. She tightly squeezes her eyes shut; all in the hopes of hearing what is being said.

That sounds like blabbering Mary Rose Mitchell. She thinks she is so beautiful. And why the heck is she sitting with Chloe? Chloe is my best friend, or so I thought. Mary Rose Mitchell, you think that you're sooo perfect. Yuck!

The whispers continue. I think those girls are talking about me. She picks out Mary Rose's voice. Her words prickle her ears. "Did you get a look at her nose."

All of a sudden there is an explosion of laughter.

Now they are laughing at me!

2

Emma can feel her face sizzle, and her eyes begin to burn. She kicks the bottom of the seat in front of her. Wham. Wham. She kicks hard. Mr. Norris looks up into his rear-view mirror. He must have heard me.

"Come on, Tuba, give us all a break," Jake says. "No honking in close quarters."

Is that what all the noise was about? Tuba must have let go of one of his foul farts. Emma brushes away her tears and dares to turn to get a quick glance. Mary Rose is pinching her nose. The boys are waving at the air in front of them. Theodore Maxwell Kart, better known as Tuba, is looking out the window with a little chipmunk grin on his face. His brown curly hair tops off his round basketball head. Emma watches him give his thick black glasses a push up the bridge of his big bulb nose. This is something that he does about every two minutes. Tuba doesn't reply. He doesn't even acknowledge the others. Hmm, he might even be happy with the attention that he's getting. He just sits there looking out the window with that little chipmunk grin.

Emma's shoulders fall into a relaxing slump. But I did hear whispers, and I heard my name.

The bus slows as it inches to the corner of Deer Haven Lane. The large doors whine open. Mary Rose bounces down the aisle tossing her long blond hair. Her tiny black skirt is a contrast to her hot pink shirt.

No, hot pink sneakers to match! Who does that? Yuck.

Mary Rose makes a sudden turnaround, grasping something in her hand. She bops back to Chloe. "Oops, I almost forgot, girlfriend. Here is my number. Give me a shout out this weekend. See ya, girlfriend."

Mary Rose breezes past Emma giving her a sneer.

Emma feels her face redden once again, and she wants to gag.

Mary Rose Mitchell, you turn my stomach. Yuck.

The bus seems to grow quieter like it does out at Pop's farm as dusk nears on a warm summer night. Emma hears Jake's laughter. She turns and sees his dimpled smile as he laughs and jokes with friends – so many friends. There is Chloe looking like she is studying the crumpled piece of paper in her hand. Emma turns back. I wonder if she's mad at me. Maybe I should have sat with her in the library yesterday. Or could it be because I didn't say something about her part in the school play? I should have made a big deal about it. I should have at least told her that she did a good job. What's wrong with you, Emma? You are such a dork.

The bus slowly turns down Morgan Road. It was named that because of the once-famous Standish Morgan Horse Farm that occupied almost the entire road. Emma and her family live in the small tenant house that was once a part of the farm. The bus wheels hum. Emma's feelings begin to warm her.

Mr. Norris always takes her road pretty slow. Emma doesn't know if it is because the road is in such desperate need of repair or because it is just so beautiful. It isn't fresh and new like Deer Haven Lane, but it's rather like the old chest that's tucked away in Gram's attic. Emma finds comfort rummaging through its contents – yellowed photos, letters written in cursive, and even a lock of her mom's baby fine hair. Emma takes in a deep breath. She even loves the musty smell of Gram's attic just like she enjoys the smell of her old country road.

Huge maple trees line both sides of the road as if they are giant tin soldiers guarding its occupants.

The remains of a tired, old, split-rail fence, practically bare of its paint, sprouts among the weeds. Emma remembers slipping off that old fence many years ago when she was pretending to ride a galloping horse. A smile curls on her face when she remembers how Jake ran over to her to see if she was ok. Yeah, he is an alright brother.

Emma can almost hear the occasional wildflowers call out to her – pick me, pick me. To this day, Emma likes to surprise Mom with a fistful of wildflowers in a rainbow of colors. Not a fancy place but a peaceful place. Almost home.

Jake gets up from his seat, making his way to the front of the bus. He must be in one big hurry. His fat, black backpack gets Emma in the shoulder, but she says nothing. She stands up. As she turns to grab her backpack, her eyes lock with Chloe's. Emma's eyes drop,

and she quickly turns away. I guess maybe I'm just not pretty enough.

Mr. Norris crawls to a stop. The doors squeal open.

Jake gives the bus driver a high five. "See ya, Mr. Norris."

"Have a good weekend, kids."

With a hanging head, Emma walks down the steps without saying a word.

Chapter 2

Home

Ok, so this isn't some fancy, dancy White House type of place with its big pillars, like the one Mary Rose lives in, but it sure isn't boring either. Our sun-yellow house looks happy and bright. Even though it has white shutters on the upstairs and downstairs windows, at least the whole thing isn't stuffy white. And the green door – it is so welcoming even if it's used just for visitors. Who cares if the front porch slants a little? Mom's colorful flowers do a great job covering the slant. Mom talks about character. Yeah, our house has character. So there, Mary Rose.

Emma continues to take her time walking up the long driveway with her backpack swung over her right shoulder.

I kinda hope it rains tonight.

Both Emma and Jake enjoy snuggling in the old, white wicker rockers placed in their own particular spot on the front porch. They like to listen to the spring geese coming in announcing that school is almost over. The chirping of the summer katydids is fun to listen to, and the flashing of the lightning bugs are fun to count. If they are really lucky, they might get to sit and watch a lightning storm without getting wet.

They head for the side door. Jake is way in the lead. Without a bark, Molly, their golden lab, comes prancing up from the back yard. Her head bobs from side to side, and her tail does a dance of its own as she runs up to greet them. Molly always seems to know when Jake and Emma get home.

Jake is the first to walk in. Emma holds the screen door open for Molly and then lets it slam shut behind her. Jake's backpack falls to the laundry room floor, almost tipping over Molly's water bowl.

Emma does not let that pass. "Jake, can't you watch what you're doing?" Molly looks up like she recognizes a stern voice. "It's ok girl."

Molly begins to take a drink.

Jake takes a step back, holding his hands up. "Whoa, excuse me!"

Emma carefully places her own backpack on the clothes dryer. She is especially careful with it. Emma bought it with her own birthday money about a month and a half ago over the Internet. Mostly she likes that it is personalized; her name in bright pink, fancy letters intertwine the glittery peace sign. It pops out against the shiny purple pack. Pink and purple are Emma's favorite colors. And her backpack has pockets, so many pockets! Emma sometimes loses things in those pockets.

"Mom, hey Ma. Mom, ya home?"

"Jake, duh ya think that she just might be out in the backyard?"

"Oh yeah. Right. That's where Molly came from. Do ya want a glass of milk, Em?" Emma walks to the kitchen cupboard. "I guess. I'll grab a couple of glasses."

"Do ya think Mom hid some cookies somewhere? Maybe in the... Oh darn!" Jake drops the milk container losing half of its contents onto the floor.

"Nice move, Jake. Now you can clean it up."

"And who said that I wouldn't?" Molly comes prancing over. "Hey, look at that. I guess that I don't have to clean it. Looks like good ole Molly's got it covered." Jake scratches the top of her nose as she laps up the milk. "What a good girl, aren't ya, Molly?"

Then Jake stands up straight and looks squarely at Emma. "So, what's your problem, Em? It seems like you've been barking ever since we got off the bus. Are you in a mood or what?"

"And why wouldn't I be? Just the whole entire bus was talking about me."

Jakes's face brightens as he pulls open the so-called 'junk drawer'. "Oh yeah, what do we have here – a package of Oreos! What the heck are you talking about, Em?"

"I heard that Miss Mary Rose say my name, and I heard the whole entire bus laughing at me."

Jake's right thumb finds his jean pocket. "You're kidding me, right?"

With her hands on her hips, Emma says, "Really, Jake? Do you think I'd be kidding about that?"

"Well, you're wrong, Em. Mary Rose was talking about that new girl in fourth grade. I think her name is Gemma or something like that. And the only person that people were laughing at was Tuba." Jake gives his head a quick shake. "Seriously, Em, what's your problem?"

"You wouldn't understand. Everyone likes you, and you have a ton of friends."

"Well, you **do** have to work at it, Em. You can't just sit in the front of the bus all by yourself. You have to put yourself out there."

Emma looks to the floor. "Easy for you to say."

"It hasn't always been easy for me. I remember hiding out in the coat closet when I was in first grade."

"Really?"

"Yeah. Some older kid was teasing me about a shirt that I was wearing on the bus ride to school one morning. I didn't know who the kid was." Jake reaches for more cookies. "Now I don't even remember the shirt. I just remember him laughing at me. So, I hid out in the coat closet; that is until the teacher came and got me." Jake chuckles and pops another cookie into his mouth.

"Jake, you better not eat them all. Mom's going to be mad." Emma takes an Oreo for herself. "Ya know, it doesn't seem like anyone cares about me. I thought that Chloe was my best friend and that I could count on her. Now she is friends with that Mary Rose. Chloe just about ignored me all day long."

"I know someone that is interested in you, but it isn't a girl."

"Yeah right."

"Really."

"Let me guess – it's Tuba?" Emma says this with a wrinkle of her nose.

Jake slowly stretches out his words. "Well, I guess that it could be Tuba."

"Figures."

Jake points a gotcha finger at Emma. "But it's not."

The side door bangs shut. Mom bounces in. She drops her gardening gloves onto the washer. She unlaces her dirt-caked sneakers, leaving them by the door. Emma notices beads of sweat on her forehead.

"Hi, guys. Did you have a good day at school? Ok, Jake, who found the cookies?"

He tips his head sideways and gives a dimpled grin. "It must have been Molly."

"Jake, please put them away – NOW!"

"Ok, Mom, but you know that I'm a growing boy."

Mom pulls the band from her ponytail, and her brown sun-streaked hair falls to her shoulders. She plants a kiss on the top of Emma's head. "How's my girl?"

Jake mutters dropping one word after the other, "I don't think that you really want to ask that question."

Emma's eyes quickly shift to the floor, and her mouth tightens. "Let's just say that I'm glad that it's Friday."

"Ya know it's going to be a busy weekend. Jake, you'll have to ask Dad to take you to ball practice in the morning. I have to make cupcakes for the bake food sale." Jake moves the cookies from the table to the counter while sneaking two more. "Emma, while I'm helping out at the sale, you can walk to the library and return the books. We'll get groceries when we're done. And both of you need to clean your rooms!"

Jake groans, "Geez, Mom, I just cleaned my room a week ago."

Mom points a finger. "You listen to me, Jake. Your room looks like it has imploded. In fact, you might just want to get started now because I can guarantee that it's going to take you more than a day to clean up that mess. Who spilled the milk?"

"Molly," Jake says with that dimpled grin.

Emma quickly shoots back, "Really, Jake? Don't believe him, Mom. You know that he blames poor Molly for absolutely everything."

"Molly knows that I love her. Don't ya girl." Jake briskly rubs Molly's head.

"Listen, we're done here. You two can both go upstairs and get changed." Take your backpacks with you when you go. And please, if anyone has homework to do, don't wait until Sunday night to get started with it." Mom picks up her gardening gloves and grabs her sneakers. "I have just a little more work to do in the backyard before I get dinner started. Let's go, Molly. You can come with me. Jake and Emma don't need any distractions. They have work to do."

"Race ya, Em."

"Ya, whatever."

Chapter **3**

Negotiations

Emma scans Jake's room to find a place to sit down. With the tips of two fingers, she picks up a pair of dirty gym shorts from the desk chair. She drops them to the floor.

"Geez, Jake, I can see what Mom was talking about. There's not even a place to sit!" She leans into the desk only to find her elbow in a sticky mess. "Yuck! How long has this funky peanut butter and jelly sandwich been laying around here?"

With one arm, Jake sweeps the stuff laying on top of his bed all the way to the bottom of the bed. Now he has enough room to plop down. His head rests in his cradling hands.

"Listen, Em, no one asked you to sit down, and you can leave if you don't like it. I'm quite comfortable here."

"You don't have to get all defensive. But how do you find anything?"

Jake looks at Emma. "I know right where everything is."

"Hey, that's a nice racecar poster. Is that the one I gave you for Christmas?"

"No. I've had it." Jake picks up a damp bath towel that he has been half laying on and flings it to Emma. "Em, toss this towel in the bathroom, will ya?"

Emma exits the bedroom with the towel in hand. "Oh, this will make a big improvement." Emma quickly returns with a question on the tip of her tongue. She slowly gets it out. "So, Jake, this person that's interested in me, are you going to tell me who it is?"

Jake sits up. "Now I get it. That's why you're being so nice to me and hanging around with my so-called mess and all."

"Well, yeah, I would like to know."

"Guy talk, Em."

"Guy talk?" Emma's voice begins to climb. "I'm your sister, and you know what I've been going through. Besides, you know that I would tell you if you were in my shoes. Please, Jake."

"Well, if you really want to know that bad. But you do know that it's going to cost ya."

"Cost me! Cost me what?"

Jake taps the calendar hanging next to his bed. "I'm really busy this weekend, and I know how good you are at cleaning your room."

Emma puts her hands on her hips. "You've got to be kidding me."

"Em, really, do I look like I'm kidding?"

Emma holds both hands out as she scans left to right. "Jake, look at this room. Just *look* at it. I could really get lost in this mess."

Jake stands and lifts both his shoulders and hands. "Hey, that's fine. It's totally up to you."

Emma spots something amongst the heap on the desk. "Jake, I've been looking all over for those headphones. No wonder I couldn't find them."

"Should've asked."

"Ok, so what if I **help** you clean your room?"

"That doesn't sound much like a deal to me, Em. I'd probably end up doing almost all of it by myself."

"Come on Jake. Some stuff I probably wouldn't even know what it was. I don't have a clue where your things belong. Then you wouldn't be able to find anything. You'd probably get all mad. It would be impossible!"

Tapping his calendar once again, Jake says, "Ok, so you can help me clean my room for a month."

Chicken-like, Emma sticks out her neck and raises her voice. "A month! You're definitely kidding me? How about two weeks?"

"Em, it's a month," Jake says, shaking his head from side to side. "You can take it or leave it. It's totally up to you."

"Fine. I'll do it. So, Jake, who is it?"

"Pete."

"Pete? Not Pete Tarino?"

"I don't know about you, but I only know just one Pete."

"You mean dreamy, black hair, green eyes, funny, sports star Pete?"

"Listen Em, Pete isn't the only sports star in school and something tells me that I'm going to regret this."

Just like popcorn kernels that begin to heat up, Em's body begins to stir. "So, what happened? What did he say?"

Jake leans against his closet door. He slaps the air with the back of his hand. In a matter -of- fact way he says, "It was nothing. No big deal. Just like I said, guy talk."

Emma's hands find her hips. "Jake, it is a big deal to me. If I'm going to help you clean up this disaster for a whole month then you have to tell me the whole complete story from beginning to end."

"Like I said, it was nothing. We were walking by the gym when you were having class, and he said that I have a cute sister. That's it."

"Cute?"

"Em, that's what he said. He used the word cute."

"Pete Tarino thinks that I'm cute!" Emma twirls herself in a circle.

"Yep, big mistake." Jake plops himself back onto his bed. "And if you're going to keep twirling around in my room then you can leave now before you break something or mess something up."

"Pete Tarino thinks that I, Emma Lee Wright, am cute. I just don't believe it!"

"You can close the door behind you." Jake's voice is stern. "And don't forget our deal."

Emma just about floats down the hall to her own bedroom. Standing in front of the oval mirror, part of the antique bedroom set given to her by her grandmother, she brushes her hair.

Emma, maybe you don't look so bad after all. My hair isn't blond and bouncy like Mary Rose's hair but it's not perfectly straight either. Brown with a little body – like Mom's hair. People say that I look like Mom, and that's a good thing. Emma steps a little closer to the mirror. A few freckles – I guess they're ok. My teeth look good. Mom was right about the braces. My nose? I wish that I had Jake's nose, but I don't think that it is anything to laugh at. Pete Tarino. Am I dreaming or what? Emma smiles. I can't believe that Pete thinks that I'm cute. So there, Mary Rose. I think I'll change and walk to the woods.

Emma is out the side door, hopping off the step. She skips over to Mom. "Hey Mom, this looks really nice. You've sure been pulling a bunch of weeds."

On her knees over a bed of pink tulips, Mom straightens up while arching her back. Her face is puzzled as she looks at Emma. "What's come over you? Emma, you *can't* be the same girl that I just saw in the kitchen."

Emma picks up an armful of weeds and places them in the wheelbarrow. "What do ya mean, Mom?"

"Since when have you ever noticed weeds? You just seem a whole lot happier than you did a few minutes ago. Is there something in those Oreos that I don't know about, or do you just want something?"

"Like I said, it's the weekend. Mom, I've got this project for school, and I thought that I would walk to the woods to collect some leaves."

"Well, I'm glad that you're not waiting till the last minute to do homework, but you really don't have to walk to the woods." Mom sweeps her right hand from left to right. "We have plenty of leaves around here."

"But there's more variety in the woods."

Mom's attention goes back to the tulips. "Does your brother have any homework?"

"Don't know, but his room is sure a mess."

Mom shakes her head. "Emma, you don't have to tell me that. If you're going to go to the woods, I don't want you to be gone long. I'll be starting dinner in about ten minutes, and your father should be home any time now. And be sure to take Molly with you."

Sniffing amongst the flower beds, Molly immediately picks her head up and wags her tail when she hears her name.

"Sure thing, Mom."

Emma pats her knee. "Come on, Molly. Let's go, girl."

Chapter **4**

The Woods

Emma just loves the woods. Mom used to read to Emma and Jake just about every night before bed when they were little. Not so much anymore. Mom says that they are old enough to read to themselves. But Mom does make exceptions with books that are long like the Harry Potter series. Then the three of them take turns reading a page or two. Well, Mom does read more pages than Emma or Jake. Still, Emma misses being read to. And it seems like all of Emma's favorite stories, the ones that she longs to hear, again and again, take place in the woods. To Emma, the woods are a place that holds magic and promise.

Just imagine finding a house made entirely out of candy! Yum. But bumping into a wicked witch, that's another story. Hansel and Gretel remain one of Emma's favorites, but still, she gets a little scared inside when she reads it. She imagines Jake as Hansel and herself as

Gretel. The witch tries to plump Jake up before eating him. Naw, Mom and Dad would never let that happen to them.

What about Goldilocks and the Three Bears? Wouldn't it be neat to meet a family of bears? They were such a nice family and cute too.

Whenever Emma visits the woods, she keeps her eyes open for dwarfs. She figures that if Snow White could find them, then she could too. What great fun would it be to live in a house with dwarfs!

Yes, Emma just loves the woods. She and Jake have had some great times exploring and adventuring together. And sometimes it's the go-to place when she wants to disappear or just be alone. There are times when she has to get away from Jake or even Mom for that matter.

Not Dad, though, as he's not around that much. When Emma is in the woods, her problems seem to melt away and nothing else matters.

To get to the woods, Emma has to cross a long alfalfa field. She likes it when the plants are covered with tiny purple flowers. Their sweet smell reminds her of Gram's hand lotion. But when they have their flowers, it means that the plants are tall and ready for cutting. It makes it difficult to walk through. Emma lifts her legs high, almost to her chest; first one and then the other. She imagines herself in a marching band. Molly excitedly bounds ahead of her. Her tail wags high, like the baton of the drum majorette, leading the coming attraction.

They reach the woods. Emma stops to rest at its edge. She sits on a familiar boulder, which has soaked up the sun's warmth. Molly doesn't wait. She is just too excited. She runs into the woods ahead of her.

Emma remembers that she doesn't have much time to spend. Mom is probably getting dinner ready by now.

Ok, so the assignment is to find two different kinds of plant leaves. The plants with opposite leaves should be easy enough to find. I don't know about the alternative leaves though. I'm not quite sure what that means.

Emma gives the passing plants a nudge with her foot. I think that they will be easier to find if I go further into the woods. More choices.

Just then Emma hears the sound of a bird overhead. She stops. It isn't the singing that she hears from the bird choir that occupies the willow tree in her backyard. It is more of a screeching sound. Emma knows that this bird is giving a warning to the others that an intruder has entered their sanctuary.

Emma doesn't like feeling as if she is an intruder like she sometimes feels at school. After all, she loves these woods and feels so at home here. She continues to walk on.

Emma notices that the leaves under her feet have lost their crunch. Probably because of the winter's wet, heavy snow. Things look so much different than they did just a few short months ago. The last time she was in the woods, she was dodging snowballs thrown by Jake. She vaulted from one tree to the other, using each for cover. Now she walks alone as streaks of sunlight sidestep the fresh, fluttering spring leaves, dancing about her as they reach the ground.

So, beautiful!

Emma moves further into the woods.

Molly? Where did that dog go? Emma resists calling. She doesn't want to break the silence.

Hmm, what's that over there?

Emma walks to a bit of a clearing to find a junk pile.

I don't think that we've seen this pile before. She begins to rummage through it with her foot. Emma likes to go bottle hunting with Mom. Mom told her that years ago people would take their trash to the woods. Talk about pollution! Mom has a nice collection of bottles, all shapes, and sizes. She has a few different colors too. The trouble is that you can never really get the bottles clean. I guess that helps them to look old. Maybe I can find a bottle for Mom.

Emma spots a long, thick stick nearby. Bending down, she picks it up and starts rummaging through the pile.

What's this? A pair of broken eyeglasses. She lifts the glasses to her face. Boy, they're weird looking.

Hey, I saw an old metal pot like this at Gram's house. Using the stick, she rubs some of the dried mud off of it. I like the blue speckles, but this is one is mostly rust. She drops the pot

Just to check in, Molly comes strolling by. "Hey, where've you been, girl?" Emma strokes Molly's back as Molly's wet nose bumps Emma's cheek. Molly is quickly off again sniffing some nearby trees. "You stay here, girl. We'll be going soon."

Emma continues rummaging. What's this? It's smooth and bluish-green. That's a good sign. Emma recognizes the color. She begins to dig with the tip of her stick. It is easy digging because the soil is so moist. She begins to feel excited as she continues to dig around the object.

Maybe I can pull it out now. Yes! Mom's going to love this, and it's not broken a bit. She holds it up high to admire it.

Emma takes the bottle to show Molly her find. She sits against one of the trees that Molly has been sniffing. She carefully begins to rub the mud off the bottle, this time with her hand. The bottom is square, and it has a rather long round neck. Emma turns the bottle upside down and begins to shake the dirt out of it. Neat! There is even raised lettering on the bottom. I know Mom doesn't have one like this. I wonder what it says. The bluish-green bottles are my favorite.

Molly begins to prance around Emma. "Hey, Molly, what are you all excited about? Did you find something, girl?"

Emma stands as she carefully puts her newly found treasure into the plastic bag that she pulls from her back jeans pocket. She ties the bag to her belt loop.

"Hey, you!"

What was that? Emma quickly scans the woods that surround her.

It is a low, slow, gruff voice, "Yeah, I'm talking to you girl."

"Molly, runnn!"

Chapter **5**

Escape

Which way? Which way do I go? Someone or something besides me and Molly is in the woods, and we gotta get out of here. Geez, what is that? Where is it hiding?

Molly, standing a few yards ahead of Emma, stops and peers behind her. Molly's tail is wagging! Emma races up to her and gives her a swat on the behind.

"Molly, don't stop. Go, girl. Go!" Molly turns and takes off.

Emma is frightened and confused. She feels a pulsing in her head and has lost all sense of direction. Is this the way out? No, this doesn't look right.

I think it's more to the left.

Emma doesn't dare stop to get her bearings. Could she possibly be running further *into* the woods? Did she hear that ugly sound again?

"Home, Molly, let's go home, girl."

Emma has to put all of her faith in Molly if she wants to get out of this mess. Molly stops and looks at Emma for just a moment. She understands. Molly takes off like a whizzing arrow with her tail resembling just that. She is soon way ahead of Emma who is having a hard time keeping her eyes on her.

Emma watches as Molly glides over a fallen log.

The ground, I have to pay attention to… Umph! Too late. Emma trips over a tree root and falls onto the glass bottle. It doesn't break.

Molly must sense that something is wrong. She stops and looks back at Emma.

Emma must convince herself that she can do this. Get up, Emma. You're ok. That thing just might be following you. You can't stop now. As soon as Emma scrambles to her feet, Molly takes off again.

The boulder! Yes, I see it. That's the boulder up ahead.

Emma hollers out to Molly, "We're almost there! Keep going, girl!"

Emma finally reaches the boulder and leans against it, trying to catch her breath. The boulder has lost some of its warmth. She hears thumping. It feels as if Emma's heart is about to thump right out of her chest. She listens intently for any unusual sound. She hears only the gentle breeze. The birds have grown quiet. Emma keeps her eyes on the woods scanning from left to right. She sees nothing out of the ordinary. Yet the woods – it looks so different now.

Molly? Where has she gone to now? Emma spots a small rock pile edging the woods, and there is Molly nesting in the tall grass with the slipping sun above her.

"Molly, what are you doing over there? Come on girl. Let's go home." In a flash, Molly is by her side.

Emma begins to cross the field. She is tired and still panting. The alfalfa grabs at her feet, trying to hold them down. But she has to pick her legs up high if she wants to get home. It is a struggle. The marching band is surely gone.

No. The sun is beginning to fall behind the trees. I wonder what time it is. How long have I've been gone?

Just then Emma sees a figure in a distance up ahead. Is that Jake coming towards her? Yes, it is Jake! Emma has never been so happy to see him. She wants to run toward him, but all of her strength has been left in the woods. When they finally reach each other, Emma falls into him with a hug. With a scrunched-up face, Jake brushes her off.

"Emma, where the heck have..."

"Jake, there is something in the woods. I heard it, and it was chasing me."

"What are you talking about, Emma? Do you have any idea what time it is?"

Emma grabs the dangling bottle from her side. "Jake, I was just cleaning off this old bottle that I found for Mom, and I heard this ugly deep voice. It sure didn't sound like a dwarf to me. More like a troll."

Jake chuckles while running his hand through his hair. "Emma, you're going to need more than that old bottle when you get home and see Mom."

"Jake, it isn't a bit funny. Did you hear anything that I said? Something was chasing me."

Jake gives a nod. "Yeah, I know. It was a big, ugly troll. But don't they live under bridges, Em?"

"You can laugh all you want, but I know what I heard."

A furrow crosses Jake's brow. "Well, did you see anything?"

"After I heard its ugly voice, I sure wasn't going to stick around to see anything."

"What about Molly?"

Tired of these questions, Emma lifts her shoulders and sounds a bit annoyed. "What do you mean about Molly?"

Putting his hands into his pockets, Jake replies. "Well, did she bark or anything?"

Emma answers quickly and firmly. "No, but when I told her to run she ran, and she ran ahead of me."

"Emma, of course, Molly is going to run if you tell her to." Holding his hands out as if he's giving a gift, Jake says, "Don't you remember how crazy Molly acted when the UPS guy came to drop off your backpack? She would have at the very least barked if something were in the woods. She probably would have freaked out."

"Yeah but…"

Jake gives a slight shake of his head. "Emma, maybe you read just way too many fairytales."

Emma relaxes just a bit. Still grasping her bagged bottle, she lets it fall back to her side. "Well, I guess it is kind of funny that Molly didn't bark."

Jake turns and begins to walk away with Emma following. "I tell ya, we got to get home. Dad called and said that he's going to be late. Mom's not happy with that. Then you're late. When you see Mom, you might just wish that you ran into a troll. We're all done with dinner."

Emma steps closer. "I'm super glad that you came to find me, Jake."

"Yeah, well, Mom made me," Jake says with a glance back at her. "And one more thing, Em, hugs are totally off-limits."

Chapter **6**

Discussion

Hoping to sneak into the house, Emma slowly and quietly opens the side screen door. It squeaks.

Jake follows, announcing their return. "Hey Ma, we're home."

Emma shoots Jake a dirty look.

There Mom stands, with her hands on her hips, right smack dab in the kitchen doorway. She does not look happy. "Emma Lee Wright, where in the world have you been?"

Jake chimes in, "Can you believe getting chased by trolls"

"Listen, Jake, this is between your sister and me," Mom says with her finger-pointing. "I think that you should just keep out of this. In fact, I think that you should go and clean your room or start your homework. Your choice."

Jake heads for the stairs in a huff with heavy feet. "Fine but I didn't do anything."

Mom stands solid. "Emma?"

Emma knows that she is in big trouble and her eyes begin to burn. "Mom, I didn't mean to be so late. I walked to the woods, and before I could find any leaves, I found this old junk pile." Emma begins to fidget with her bagged bottle. "So, I found a stick and started digging through the pile and..."

Mom holds up one finger, and her voice begins to climb. "Wait a minute. Just wait a minute, Emma. Do you mean to tell me that you've been gone all this time, and you didn't even collect your leaves?"

Emma's eyes fall to the floor while her voice speeds up. "Well nooo. But Mom, I found this great bottle and I know that you don't have one like it. Then I heard this really weird noise. And then..."

Mom speaks with measured words. "Listen, Emma, I appreciate that you were thinking of me. It's nice that you found the bottle, but there is something bigger here. I told you that I was just about ready to get dinner started, and I asked that you not be gone long. We've been waiting for you and your father to have dinner. Jake and I finally ate without both of you. When you still didn't come home, I started to get concerned."

"I didn't mean to be late."

"Emma, you have to be responsible. Your dinner is in the microwave. When you're done, please clean up your dishes. Then you can go to your room"

Brushing a tear from her eye, Emma murmurs, "Sorry, Mom."

Emma has her dinner and cleans her mess. She heads upstairs and stops at Jake's closed door. Knocking, she says, "Can I come in?"

"Whatever."

She steps in. "What are you doing, Jake?"

Without taking his eyes off his tablet, he answers, "Trying to beat my score."

"Jake, sorry you had to come upstairs. I didn't mean to get you in trouble."

"Yeah, this really stinks. Here it is on a Friday night and we're stuck upstairs in our rooms. Maybe Mom just wanted to have the TV to herself. Dad should be home soon, and you know how they like to have their alone time. Maybe that's what it is."

A tiny flash catches the corner of Emma's eye. "Hey, I see something under your desk. What is that?"

Jake pops up from his bed with his tablet still in hand. He peers under his desk. "Oh yeah!" He drops to his knees and quickly retrieves a shiny coin. "This is the baseball coin that I've been looking for." Jake stands and slowly inspects the coin, flipping it from one side to the other. "I've looked all over the place for this." He shakes it in front of Emma. "Ya know, this is my lucky charm. Thanks, Em."

Emma restlessly twirls a strand of her hair. "Yeah, whatever. I sure could use a lucky charm." With magnified eyes, she slowly begins to stammer. "Ya know, Jake, you can't even guess how good it was to see you walking across that field. I really did hear something weird in the woods, and I really thought that I was done for."

"Like I said, it couldn't have been anything too big or Molly would have gone crazy. It was probably just your imagination or maybe the wind."

"The wind wasn't blowing, but you are right about Molly. Emma looks with pleading eyes. "Jake, would you go back to the woods with me?"

Jake continuously flips his baseball coin and catches it every time. "If I were you, Em, I wouldn't even think of going back to the woods anytime soon. You're just lucky that Dad isn't home. Besides I'm busy tomorrow. And remember, you've got my room to clean."

Emma sticks out her chicken neck and puts her hands on her hips. "Really? You don't have to keep reminding me about your room, Jake. Besides, how could I forget? All I have to do is walk by your door." Emma turns and stomps to her own room.

Jake calls out, "Oh yeah, that friend of yours called while you were gone. Chloe, I think."

Discussion

Emma quickly returns to Jake's door, and her voice begins to bubble. "Chloe called? What time did she call?"

"It was before dinner."

"Jake, why didn't you tell me? It could be important."

Jake stops flipping his coin and looks directly at Emma. "Why didn't I tell you? When? It seems like we've been a little busy around here, Em."

"I got to talk to Mom."

"Lots of luck with that." Jake continues to flip his coin.

Emma hurries down the steps and finds Mom sitting at the kitchen table with a magazine in front of her. "Mom, can I talk to you?"

Mom looks up from her magazine. "Yes. What is it, Emma?"

"Jake just told me that Chloe called when I was gone. Can I call please call her back?"

"No, absolutely not," Mom says, shaking her head.

Emma's words race out. "But Mom, it's probably really important. Maybe she wants us to get together tomorrow. Maybe she wants me to go to her house."

"Emma, you should have been home to take the phone call yourself. You can return her call when we get back tomorrow afternoon."

"But it might be too late by the afternoon and if I had a cell phone…"

"**Enough**. I said no phone call tonight. That's it."

Emma turns and walks away with a stomp.

Chapter 7

The Phone Call

"Hi Mrs. Anderson, this is Emma Wright. Chloe called me last night and I'm returning her phone call. Is she busy?"

Emma is anxious to hear what this is all about, and she can hear Chloe being called to the phone. Oh good! She must be home.

Just in case she has to take a note, Emma has a pad and pencil ready. While waiting, she taps the eraser to the pad.

Chloe is a girl that everyone wants to be friends with. Her long, black, straight hair seems to frame her pretty face. Emma thinks that she is Pocahontas-like. Besides that, she is kind, soft-spoken and always seems to say the right thing. Chloe is the ultimate friend; that is unless Mary Rose has her claws gripped into her.

"Hi, Emma. How's it going?"

"Great, Chloe. Sorry it took so long for me to get back to you. I was out last night, and it was late by the time Jake told me that you called. You know how boys are. You're lucky that you don't have a brother to deal with."

Chloe giggles. "Em, your brother is cute, and he was so nice on the phone."

The tapping stops, and Emma begins to doodle. "Yeah, I guess that he's ok as far as brothers go. Anyway, it was late last night, and this morning I had to go to the bake food sale with Mom."

"Oh, did you see Mary Rose? She said that she might work at the sale today."

The doodling stops and dark, frowning faces appear. "No, I didn't see Mary Rose, but Stephanie was there. She was packaging up cookies. Actually, I didn't help that much. I walked to the library to return some books. So, anyway I was wondering why you called."

"Well, if you're not busy this afternoon, Maddy and I were wondering if you would like to go shopping with us. We thought that we would go and get a birthday gift for Mary Rose's party. We talked about maybe chipping in together and getting her a bigger gift."

Chloe's voice seems to trail off into the distance. Emma presses the pencil tip hard into the paper – so hard that it snaps. "Sorry, Chloe. I'm busy this afternoon. I promised Jake that I would help him with his room. Besides, I wasn't invited to the party."

"Oh." There is a forever pause. "I'm sorry, Emma. I didn't know." Chloe's voice softens, and it's as if it's hard for her to get the words out. "But I'll see you at school on Monday."

Emma tosses the pencil on the counter. "Ok then, see ya on Monday, Chloe." She takes her doodling paper and scrunches it in her hand. She stomps to the trash can, opens the lid, and dumps her doodles. A birthday party – unbelievable! Emma turns and storms up the stairs.

Wham. Slam. Bam, bam.

Mom calls up from the bottom of the stairs, "Emma, I think that it's great that you offered to help clean your brother's room, but do you really think that you need a bulldozer to do it? What are you doing up there?"

Emma sharply answers, "Nothing. Mom, where is Jake?"

"He's still at baseball practice. What is the problem, Emma?"

Emma pounds down the stairs. "What is the problem? What isn't a problem? Mom, you said that I could return Chloe's phone call today. So, I called. Do you know what she wanted? She wanted me to go shopping with her today."

"Well, that's nice."

"Nice? Nice? Do you know what she wanted to shop for? She thought that we might go shopping together for Mary Rose's birthday present. Yeah, birthday present.

She wanted to chip in together and get her some big gift. How embarrassing! I had to tell her that I wasn't even invited. Do you believe that? Mary Rose, yuck." Emma heads for the kitchen with Mom trailing behind.

Emma's buries her face in the kitchen table while trying to harness her sobs. Mom gently strokes her hair. "Listen to me, Emma. I know that Mary Rose isn't your favorite person. Really, what fun would it be for you to go to a party for someone that you don't especially care for?"

Emma looks up with tears falling down her scarlet face. "Mom, you don't get it. I'm probably the only one in our whole class that wasn't invited. And it's all because I'm so ugly."

With both hands, Mom softly wipes the tears away. "Emma, you know that isn't true. You need to take a breath and settle down."

Emma's voice begins to twang. "But Mom, what am I going to do? How can I even face those girls on Monday? I don't even want to go to school."

"You have so many nice girls in your class. There is Bailey, Hope, and what about Justine? There are so many good girls in your class that I can't even name them all! Now you know that they weren't all invited to the party. Maybe Mary Rose had to pick two or three of her very best friends."

"Mary Rose, yuck. Besides, Chloe is my best friend, and I'm just totally embarrassed."

"Emma, think about Chloe. I am willing to bet that she feels a bit embarrassed herself."

Words drop out in-between sobs. "Why can't I just be popular like Jake?"

"We've talked about this before. Everyone is different and special in their own way. Being the very best person that you can be is far better than being popular. That's why your father and I are so proud of you. You are such a kind and loving person." Mom gently gives Emma's nose a tap. "Even though you think Mary Rose is a bit yucky."

"But Mom, what am I going to do?" Emma's hands tighten into fists.

"Well, for now, I think that you'll feel better if you get a little exercise – maybe go for a walk or something. Then on Monday, you are going to act as though nothing is wrong, and you are going to be that very special person that we are so very proud of."

"You make it sound so easy."

"Emma, I'm not going to kid you. It won't be easy. But I know that you are a tough girl, and you will get through it. In a few weeks from now, this will all be forgotten, and there will be a new adventure."

"I guess." Emma wipes her eyes with the backs of her hands. Feeling the need to clear her head, Emma considers taking a walk to the woods. But is there a monster in the woods, or was it all her imagination?

Heck, how could things get worse? Taking a deep breath, she asks, "Mom, is it ok if I go to the woods?"

Mom answers with head down and eyes up. "Really, Emma, the woods?"

Emma's words spill out. "Well, it is good exercise. I'll take Molly with me. And, Mom, you know the woods is my favorite place to be when I'm down."

Mom gives a half-grin. "Yes, it is good exercise but aren't you afraid of running into a troll or something?"

"Funny, Mom. Anyway, after today maybe running into a troll would be a good thing. Besides, remember – I'm tough."

Mom points her finger straight at Emma and speaks firmly, "Ok, Emma, but you take your watch and be sure that you are home by four o'clock at the very latest. And don't forget to collect your leaves."

Emma lets out a breath of relief and wraps her arms around Mom's neck. "Thanks. We'll be back by four – I promise. Let's go, Molly. Come on, girl."

Chapter **8**

The Toad

With Molly trotting by her side, Emma quickly lifts one leg after the other as she crosses the alfalfa field. The grass seems to have grown a bit taller overnight.

"We don't have a lot of time Molly. I'm surprised that Mom even let us go to the woods. I thought that it might be a year or more before we saw the woods again. Yeah, we're lucky. Mom was really mad last night."

Emma begins to have second thoughts. She can hear Mom's words playing in her head. "Aren't you afraid of running into a troll or something?" Hmm, maybe this isn't such a great idea after all. Emma tries to shrug off the monster in her head. Yeah, I can do this. Besides, I don't think that my day can get any worse, troll or no troll.

Surprisingly, Molly doesn't run off. She sticks close to Emma's side. Molly always seems to know when Emma is having a bad day.

The Toad

And Mom is right about Mary Rose. Who would want to go to her dumb old party anyway? Not me. Besides, Chloe and I are good friends. She did call, and she wants to see me on Monday. She must have felt really weird when I told her that I wasn't invited to the party. It was kinda nice that she wanted me to go shopping with her; even if it was for a dumb birthday present. Yuck.

Emma and Molly are nearing the woods.

I wish Jake was here. Emma feels her stomach begin to rumble. She tries not to think of the creepy voice that she heard in the woods. She tries to keep her mind busy instead. I wonder if practice is over yet. I can't wait to see Chloe on Monday. Wait till I tell her about Pete. I wonder if he is at practice. He must be. I wonder if he talked to Jake about me. Pete Tarino, so there Mary Rose Mitchell.

Emma looks at the woods creeping up on her. I should have had Mom tell Jake to come up and meet us. Too late now.

"We can do this, Molly." With a wag of her tail, Molly looks up at Emma in agreement.

Emma's steps seem to almost bog down. To get Molly's full attention, she quickly brushes her hand on top of Molly's head. "You stay with me now, girl, ya hear. We're almost there."

As Emma scans the upcoming woods, a flash of activity catches her eyes. She stops dead in her track with the thought of turning back home. She peers intently with binocular-like eyes along the group of tall pines. Then she recognizes an occasional bobbing white tail.

Oh, it's just some deer. They're busy eating. Maybe we can sneak up on them. They look like they're guarding the woods. I wonder if woods and forest are the same. Emma continues her walk.

"Look, Molly, deer at the edge of the woods! Let's be quiet now. They don't see us yet."

With the sound of her name, Molly picks her head up. She seems to catch a scent, and then she is off in a dead heat.

"Molly! Molly, you get back here!"

I guess she saw them. Oh great. Now, what do I do? We've come too far to turn back. I have to remember, I am tough.

Emma steps up and runs after Molly.

Nearing the boulder, Emma looks down toward the pines. The only thing she sees is one long wagging tail. Molly has her head down, snuzzling the ground. There's that dog!

"Here Molly. Come on girl." Molly lifts her head and immediately comes running toward Emma. "That's right. Good girl."

Emma briskly scratches the top of Molly's head. Molly wags her tail excitedly.

Squatting to the ground, Emma holds Molly's head in her hands and speaks in a firm voice, "Listen,

Molly, I don't want you running off by yourself. You stick with me girl, ya hear? And if you see, hear, or smell anything unusual, you let me know. Do you understand, girl?" Molly gives Emma's hand a quick lick. "Ok, Molly, let's go."

Emma crosses that fine line that divides the sun-soaked field and the fortified forest. The moment she steps in, she gives a shudder. She feels a sudden chill that reaches her bones.

"I can do this."

Emma's eyes dart back and forth like the pendulum on Gram's schoolhouse clock. She scans the nearby trees. Nothing seems to be out of the ordinary. She takes a few more steps. She pauses and listens. She doesn't hear the usual warning sounds from above. That's unusual.

Emma continues to walk. She looks up. The spring leaves are peeking down at her. She sees the sunlight dodging the new growth. The birds seem to be singing their hearts out. Emma begins to relax. A smile gently brushes her face.

Walking along, Emma's hand skims Molly's back. "Remember girl, I don't want you going too far. You stay close by. And for sure, we can't be late getting home." Emma taps her back-jean pocket.

Oh darn. I forgot to bring a plastic bag.

Just ahead of Emma is a small heap. Hmm, there's that same junk pile. Emma starts to walk more to the left.

I better steer clear of that. Digging for bottles – not a good idea. Mom probably has enough anyway.

Emma heads toward a clump of trees that are surrounded by a lot of underbrush. I probably should collect my leaves first of all. There should be a lot of different kinds of leaves over here.

Emma kneels on the ground. She breaks off a stem to examine it. Opposite leaves are two leaves right across from each other on a stem. Yeah, this looks like it. That was easy. Emma gives her surroundings a quick scan. She listens for any unusual sound. Nothing. She goes back to her search. Leaves that aren't across from each other on the stem are alternate. Hmm, alternate, that sounds like it might harder to find.

Emma glances over at Molly. She is sniffing a nearby tree. Her nose is down, and her tail is up. It looks like she's on a mission. That's good. That way Emma doesn't have to worry about her going too far.

Emma goes back to her search, inspecting one plant at a time. She quickly lifts herself from her knees when she feels the dampness of the ground through her jeans. She crouches instead. Emma takes a deep breath. She likes the smell of the fallen wet leaves as she rummages through the new growth. Alternate, not across from each other. Emma yanks on the stem. Yeah, this looks like it might be one. Emma continues her search.

"Yelp!"

"What's the matter, Molly?"

The Toad

Emma stands and walks over to the nearby tree. Molly's nose is still nestled close to the ground. Her tail is still standing tall, but it has lost its wag.

"What do ya have, girl? Did a bee get ya?"

Emma spots a long, thin stick. She likes most animals, but she is not too fond of snakes. She remembers the time when Jake chased her with a brown speckled garden snake when she was about three years old. Emma doesn't want to take a chance, so she picks up the stick.

"Let me see what ya have there, girl." Emma tries to nudge Molly away from the tree, but Molly is persistent. "Let me get in there, girl."

Finally, Molly backs off.

Emma slowly begins to sweep the foliage around the base of the tree. She peers intently. Suddenly she hears a slow, low, deep wail - "Owwwww!"

Emma quickly springs back. She pauses for just a moment. "What the heck was that?"

Emma slowly creeps to the base of the tree. She gingerly bends forward. Does she dare use her hands to look? Emma hesitantly drops her stick and begins to carefully rustle the plants below. She sees it! It is a bumpy, somewhat ugly, moss-green, toad. Could it be a talking toad? No way!

Chapter **9**

Tobias

Emma holds the green leaves back as she intently stares at the toad. The words finally fall out of her mouth. "Can you talk?"

In that slow, low, deep voice the toad answers, "No, Emma. Can you?"

Emma's mind begins to race. Words did come from this toad's mouth. And how does it know my name? Is she wearing her monogrammed sweatshirt? Emma looks down. No, she is not. What exactly is happening here?

"My name – how do you know my name?"

Slowly spoken was the reply, "It is written, my dear."

Emma is stunned. What does that mean? She doesn't know what to say or what to think.

"You really should be more careful, Emma. You know, you just about took my head off with that stick. Sticks can be very dangerous."

Not really believing that she is talking to a toad, Emma stammers, "I, I'm really sorry. I didn't mean… "

"Apology accepted, but please don't do that again, my dear."

"Listen, I really don't know what to think. I mean I know that toads really can't talk. And here I am…"

One word slowly drops after the other. "Yes, things are not always as they appear to be."

Emma repeatedly blinks her eyes and gives her head a bit of a shake. What else can she do? "Am I dreaming or what?"

The toad gives a soft chuckle. "Ahh, such is life."

It suddenly becomes clear, like when the spring fog lifts over Pearl Creek and you can actually see over to the other side. "It was you! You were the one that scared me yesterday."

The toad slowly shakes his head back and forth. "Emma, Emma, I believe that it was you that frightened yourself. I merely spoke, and you ran off."

Emma scratches her head, trying to think back and remember just what happened. It's like she opened a jigsaw puzzle box. All of the pieces are scattered.

"Ah yes, often when I speak nobody listens. My dear, you didn't even give me a chance to introduce myself. Maybe you should take a lesson from good old Molly here. Molly knows a friend when she sees one."

Emma's eyes bulge and so does her voice. "You know Molly's name too!"

"Oh, Molly and I have been friends for longer than she's been running from tree to tree in these woods. Or maybe I should say this forest." He winks. "We often have fun together, playing hide-and-seek."

Forest? How does he know? I mean I just got done saying… In frustration, Emma speaks up. "What's going on here? I don't understand. I don't get it."

"Don't be alarmed, Emma. Have you ever sat on a front porch pondering the evening sky, with only the hope of seeing a comet? You may linger night after night, watching and hoping. It will appear in due time." In a rainbow fashion, his arm drifts above his head from left to right. "Yes, understanding comes in a flash; riding on the tail of a comet. Be patient, my dear."

Emma takes one, slow, backward step and then another. Again, she scratches her head.

"Uhm, I think that we better get going. It is getting kind of late."

The toad gives a slight nod. "Yes Emma, you should be on your way. It is close to four o'clock, and you did make a promise."

Again, Emma takes another backward step, not really wanting to take her eyes off this toad. She gently kneads her forehead. How does he know that?

Emma calls Molly with a tap on her knee. "Come on girl. Let's go home."

Molly bobs next to Emma, giving her hand a quick lick. In return, Molly gets a pat to the head.

"Well, I guess that I'll see you around or something."

"Yes Emma, I *will* see you again. It was my pleasure speaking to you, my dear."

"Yeah, right. It was good."

With Molly next to her, Emma feels safe enough to actually turn around and walk away. She gives her head a slight shake, trying to clear her mind. What the heck just happened here?

Suddenly there is a sound, almost like a volcanic eruption! Emma turns with a start.

At a snail's pace, he speaks. "Emma, it might be wise to take your collection of leaves with you."

Emma returns to retrieve her pile. "Oh yeah, I forgot. Thanks for reminding me."

While bending down to pick up her leaves, Emma looks at the toad. Was that another wink?

Emma stands to walk away. She says over her shoulder, "See ya around, toad."

Molly bounces happily alongside Emma, waving her tail like a banner. Emma tries to clear her head again and just doesn't know what to think. She feels like she just might be a little piece in that puzzle box.

They near the edge of the woods. Suddenly, Emma turns with a start. Loudly she yells, "Hey toad, do you have a name?"

The slow, low, deep, thunderous, reply: **"Yes. It is Tobias, Tobias the Toad."**

Chapter **10**

All in A Name

Emma crosses the forest boundary. She wonders if it is a boundary that separates what is real from make-believe. She just doesn't know what to think.

Her head feels a bit fuzzy like it was when riding home from Gram and Pop's house in the snowstorm last winter. She remembers hundreds of giant wet snowflakes smashing into the windshield on that pitch-black night. Back then, she squeezed her eyes tight for just a moment and the fuzziness was gone.

She stops and tries this once again, with no luck. Emma slowly walks on even though a part of her wants to linger behind. This is more than strange.

Molly seems to sense Emma's distress. She bops happily beside Emma. Usually, she would go bounding ahead through the tall grass.

"Molly, you didn't even bark, girl. Do you know that toad?"

They've crossed the field, and their house is just ahead. I wonder if I should tell anyone. Either they won't believe me, or they'll think I'm crazy. "What do you think, girl? Should I tell Jake about the toad? He is good at keeping secrets. Yeah, I'll tell Jake."

Emma and Molly walk through the side door, For Molly, the first stop is her water bowl. She licks her bowl dry.

Emma finds Dad standing next to the kitchen desk. He looks like he is in deep thought. "Hi, Dad."

He gives her a squeeze and a kiss on the top of her head. "Hey Sweetie, I've been missing you. We must be moving in opposite directions lately." He puts the mail that he's been rummaging through back down on the desk.

"Molly and I just got back from the woods."

"Yes, your mother told me about you and the woods. I'm glad that you've made it back home in time, even with a few minutes to spare." Dad ruffles Emma's hair. "Did you see any trolls today, Sweetie?" He gives his dimpled grin.

"Oh, I guess Mom told you." Emma turns away from Dad and turns to the faucet to wash her hands. She is feeling a little bit embarrassed. "No Dad, no trolls. I did collect my leaves though."

Emma feels Dad's warm hand on her shoulder. "Good girl, Em. Mom will be happy to hear that."

"Where are Mom and Jake, anyway?"

"Mom ran to the store to get milk for dinner, and Jake went with her. He has to pick up a piece of poster board for a project that he has to do."

"Dad, I guess I'll go upstairs and work on my leaf report for a while."

"Good idea, Em. Ya know, I think that your brother should take a few lessons from you. He seems to need a little more of a push with his schoolwork." Dad sits down and gets back to the mail.

"Will you send Jake up when he gets home? I want to show him the leaves that I've collected."

"Sure thing, Em."

A few minutes later, Emma stands in front of Gram's mirror. "Look at you, Emma Lee Wright. Are you a nut or what? Talking to a toad! You might just as well be a toad yourself."

Well, at least it is a toad and not a troll that you're talking to – just in case anyone else should ask.

Just then Emma hears clamoring on the stairs. Taking two steps at a time and talking rather loudly Jake says, "Oh, I'm just sooo lucky. I get to see Emma's cool leaf collection. Lucky, me."

"Jake, come in and close the door. I have something to tell you."

"Whoa, this sounds kinda serious!" Jake leans up against Emma's closet door.

Emma speaks as quickly as her words can escape her. "It happened again, Jake. Molly and I went to the woods, and I heard a noise again." Emma's eyebrows take a leaping jump. "Except this time, Jake, I saw it. It's a toad — a real live toad."

Jake rubs his chin and thinks for a minute. "A toad? Em, do you mean like a ribbit toad? They're all over the place."

"No, Jake. I mean like a talking toad."

Jake stands up tall. "Get out, Emma!"

"Jake, I know that this sounds crazy but it's true. He talks, and he seems to know what is going on, and he said that he's known Molly for a really long time. He even plays hide-and-seek with her."

Jake puts his hand on Emma's forehead. "Emma, are you sure that you're feeling ok?"

She smacks his hand away and leans forward. "Jake, it's true. You have to believe me."

Jake rests back against the door. His thumbs find his jean pockets. He pauses for just a moment. "Ok, Emma. So, what does this toad look like?"

"Well, he is greenish-brown, bumpy, and kind of plump. He looks like a toad, kind of ugly but with nice eyes. I guess he looks kind of cute in a strange way. He looks really old."

Jake gives one nod. "And he talks?"

"Yes, Jake. He talks. He has a really low, deep voice. He talks slowly, and he says strange things. Like I said, he seems to know things that I've done and things that I've said. He told me that I'm going to see him again."

"Well, Em, I know that you have a great imagination, but I don't know if you could dream this one up by yourself. What was Molly doing all this time?"

Emma begins to pace as she talks. "That's it, Jake. You were right. Remember how you said that Molly would get all excited if she saw something strange. I think Molly might know this toad. She didn't act strange at all. She didn't even bark. All she did was hang around. Ya see that's proof, Jake,"

Jake sweeps his hair with his right hand. "Hmm, so you think that Molly knows this toad. I don't know, Em."

"Jake, you can't tell anyone; not yet anyway. Tomorrow we can go to the woods together. Then you'll see."

"We're going to Gram and Pop's house tomorrow. Remember? And on Monday, I have practice after school."

Emma frowns, "Oh yeah, I forgot."

"So, did this toad say anything else?"

"Yes, just before I left, I asked him if he had a name. He said that his name is Tobias, Tobias the Toad."

Jake rubs his chin. "That sounds like a weird name. I've never heard that one before."

Emma's eyes open wide. "Jake, the whole thing is weird – really weird."

"I wonder if his name means anything. I know. We can look it up on the Net." Jake leaves Emma's room and returns with his tablet in hand. He sits next to Emma on her bed.

"Hey kids," Dad calls up the stairs. "Mom wants both of you to wash and come down here." Emma and Jake look at each other. "Dinner will be on the table in five."

"Ok Dad, Jake and I will be right down."

"Here we are. The Greek and Hebrew meanings for Tobias are the same." Jake turns to look at Emma. "Em, this is wild! The meaning for Tobias – 'God is good'."

Chapter **11**

One Bad Day

Emma dreads going to school this morning. She hates the thought of facing those girls. She imagines that everyone will be talking about the big birthday party coming up next weekend. It takes her forever to figure out what top to wear, and she keeps fumbling through her closet.

Mom calls up the stairs in a sing-songy voice, "It's getting late, Emma. Cereal is on the table."

Lovely, now I have to rush.

Emma picks a cream-colored hoodie and throws it on. She steps to the mirror to do her hair. She looks a little closer. I don't believe it! A pimple and on my nose of all places! This is just going to be my day. She runs a comb through her hair.

"Emma Lee, your Dad has already left for work, and I don't have time to take you to school. Let's get a move on."

Emma stomps down the stairs. I know that Mom won't buy it if I tell her I'm sick.

"Emma, I've poured your cereal. You get your things together and I'll get the milk."

"Nooo. I'm not hungry, and I can't eat." Emma feels as if she's about to pour tears. She stops stuffing things in her backpack and looks pleadingly at Mom. Feeling her face droop, she whines, "Mom, do I really have to do this?"

Jake flies by with his backpack over his shoulder. "Ma, where's my poster?"

"It's just where you left it, Jake, on the dining room table. And, Jake, please don't let Mr. Norris leave without your sister. She'll be right there."

"Will do, Ma. See ya this afternoon. Remember, I've got practice after school." Jake scoots through the kitchen. The side door slams shut.

Mom turns to Emma with a granola bar in her hand. "Here, you take this and please be sure to eat it before school starts." Emma stares at the floor. Mom gently picks her chin up. "Listen to me, Em, you are a tough girl. Try to have positive thoughts and make this thing work." Mom plants a kiss on the top of her head. "You better get going, Em, and remember that you *will* get through this."

Emma hears Mom's words, but she really doesn't feel them. Not wanting to leave the safety of her home, she picks up her shiny purple backpack and heads to the door. In a voice that can hardly be heard, she says, "Love ya, Mom."

Emma stuffs the granola bar in the back pocket of her jeans. She scuffs down the driveway. I really don't want to do this.

All of a sudden, she sees the big yellow school bus come to a rolling stop. Jake takes a leap up the steps.

I have to hurry but I don't want to run. Those girls are probably watching me.

Emma finally gets there, and she looks to the ground as she begins to climb the steps.

"Mornin, Emma. I see that you're still looking for that lost smile of yours. Hope you find it soon — such a pretty smile."

Emma looks up at Mr. Norris and forces a half-grin. He gives her a twinkly wink.

In almost a whisper, Emma says, "Thanks, Mr. Norris."

Just as Emma steps in, she hears a soft voice from the middle of the bus. Chloe is patting the brown, vinyl seat next to her. "Here, Emma, I saved a seat for ya."

Emma's face immediately breaks into a smile. Maybe this isn't going to be such a bad day after all.

The morning bus rides to school are usually pretty quiet. Most of the kids are not fully awake. This ride is no different. Emma and Chloe talk quietly between themselves, but Emma senses that someone is listening to their conversation. Mary Rose is sitting in the seat that is across the aisle from them.

Emma touches Chloe's wrist. "That's such a pretty bracelet, Chloe. I love the leather band."

"Oh, thanks, Emma. I bought it when I went shopping with Madigan on Saturday."

Then Chloe leans to whisper into Emma's ear, but Chloe's words begin to quickly fade into space. Emma can feel a stare burning a hole into her. She turns and sees Mary Rose shooting her a dirty look.

Mr. Norris pulls into the school turnabout. Everyone takes their time gathering their things, stepping into the aisle, and filing out of the bus. The backs of Emma's legs are getting nudged with a backpack. This is not an accident. It happens again. Emma turns to find a grin on Mary Rose's face. Yuck!

The start bell rings and everyone heads to their class. The morning seems to move along almost as usual. Emma often hears Pops talk about something being slower than molasses. Now Emma has an understanding of just what he means when he says that. Emma doesn't think that she has missed even one annoying tick of that classroom clock. She looks up at it again. It's eleven-forty. There are five more minutes until lunch. Whew! She brushes her forehead with her hand. The day is half over.

Just then, Emma's teacher comes up behind her and places a paper on her desk, blank side up. Oh, this must be from Friday's quiz. Emma turns her paper over. She can feel her face turn beet red. It's a seventy – a seventy on a spelling test! *I know these words.* She checks for her name on the top of the paper. *How did this happen? I don't think I've ever had anything lower than a ninety percent on a spelling test before.*

Emma quickly stuffs the paper in her desk, with the hopes that no one else has seen her score. She screams inside her head. *You are so stupid, Emma.*

The bell rings, signaling that it's lunchtime. The class bounces to their feet.

Oh good. If I hurry, maybe Chloe will want to sit with me again. Just then Emma feels a tap on her shoulder. She turns to find her teacher, Mrs. Worman, standing right behind her.

Mrs. Worman looks over the top of her glasses that are pushed down to the tip of her nose. She is an older woman, older than her mom, but she tries to act cool. With her arms crossed she says, "Emma, could I please have just a sec of your time?"

Emma looks around and sees the entire class scramble through the door. She doesn't want to stick around, even if it's just for a 'sec.' But Emma knows that she really doesn't have a choice here. Feeling fidgety she answers, "Sure, Mrs. Worman."

"Emma, I was quite surprised by your spelling test. I was wondering if something might be bothering you."

Emma shakes her head. "No, Mrs. Worman. Everything is good"

Mrs. Worman takes off her glasses and slips them to the top of her head. She peers at Emma as if she is trying to see something inside of her. "Are you sure, Emma, because you know that I am here to help?"

Looking at the clock Emma says, "Yes, I'm sure Mrs. Worman."

"Ok then, Emma. Now you go and have a nice lunch."

Emma doesn't say another word. In fact, it takes her just a 'sec' to get out the door. She finally reaches the lunchroom. This is just great. Chloe is sitting with Mary Rose. All of my friends are together, and there is no room for me. She can hear talk of Mary Rose's birthday party and about all of the fun that they are going to have. Emma might as well be on a desert island. She sits at the very end of the table and has a playful conversation with her lunch.

Thank you, Mrs. Worman, for this lovely lunch.

Emma welcomes the ring of the signaling bell. She can't get out of that lunchroom fast enough. Gym period can't be any worse than lunch. Emma is one of the first girls in the locker room. Things have got to get better.

Emma squats down to tie her sneakers. She feels a nudge at her back. Mary Rose is looming over her. Emma pops up like a jack in the box.

"Hey there, Emma, those are cute, flowery shorts you have there. Are they new?" Mary Rose says this all with a snicker on her face and then walks away.

Emma looks down. These don't look like the same pink shorts that she packed this morning. They look babyish, wrinkly, but most of all baggy. You are so ugly, Emma.

"Ok girls, we are going to have a game of dodge ball," says the gym teacher, Mr. Thornsworth. He picks two team captains.

Great, I know how this is going to play out. Just standing there, Emma begins to sweat, like an ice-filled glass on a hot summer day.

One name is called after another but not Emma's. I can't do this. Feeling and looking flushed, Emma trots up to Mr. Thornsworth. "I think I'm going to be sick."

"Emma, you don't look well. You go back to class, and we'll see if we can contact your mom."

Emma changes her clothes and then returns to her classroom. She finds Mrs. Worman sitting at her desk and looking quite pleased with herself. She looks up.

"Just as I suspected, Emma. You are not yourself. Mr. Thornsworth buzzed me and said that you're not feeling well. He is quite concerned about you. You can sit at your desk and rest. Your mom should be here in a sec."

Emma buries her face in her arms. In a sec – I just gotta get out of here!

Chapter **12**
The Rescue

The ride home from school is heavy with quiet. When they get home, Mom turns off the car and breaks the silence. "So Em, did you eat your granola bar this morning?"

Emma leans to her left. She picks up her right butt cheek and tugs at the granola bar in her back pocket. She holds up a wrinkled, smooshed bar. She says nothing.

Mom looks over at her. "Oh, Emma. What about lunch? Did you have any lunch?"

With her head down, Emma answers, "I wasn't hungry."

Mom's voice begins to sound a little frustrated. "Did you eat anything at all?"

"I had a few chips."

"A few chips, ok. Em, do you have a stomach ache?"

"No, not really."

"Sweetie, maybe you're not feeling well because you haven't eaten, especially if you played hard in gym. And chips might not be the greatest choice."

Silence –

Mom closes the car door. "Oh, look who's come to meet us. Hi, Molly. Look who I brought home."

Emma trudges past Molly into the house and unloads her things onto the top of the dryer. She slips into the kitchen chair.

Mom walks over placing her hand on Emma's forehead. "Emma, you don't have a fever. Is there something going on at school that I should know about?"

Emma drops her head to the kitchen table, burying her eyes into her arms. She begins to sob. "I should have never gotten on that bus today. I just knew it. I should have never gone to school."

"Tell me about it, Em."

Emma looks at Mom with burning eyes. "I did just like you said, Mom. This morning I walked on the bus just like nothing was wrong. I even sat down with Chloe. She was really nice to me. I thought that it was going to be a great day. Then I told her how I liked the bracelet that she was wearing. She started whispering in my ear, and do you want to know what she said? She bought the same identical bracelet as a dumb birthday present for Mary Rose. Can you believe that? Mary Rose was watching the whole time, and I think that she got jealous because she was mean to me for the whole rest of the day."

"Emma, do you think that you might be imagining some of this?"

Emma raises her voice and clenches her fist. "Mom, I am **not** imaging it, and the day just kept getting worse. I feel so left out. I was sitting at lunch by myself, and all I could hear was all those girls talking about that dumb birthday party next weekend."

"Do you mean that you heard them talking about the birthday party that you really don't want to go to?"

Emma cries all the harder as she goes through the entire day. She tries to wipe tears away, but they won't stop falling. "Mom, I am just so ugly, and I don't have any friends." Feeling exhausted, Emma drops her head to the table again and sobs in her folded arms.

Mom gently rubs Emma's back. "Listen to me, Emma Lee Wright. You are not ugly; not unless you think that I'm ugly too. And your father doesn't seem to think so. Everyone says that we look like sisters. Emma, you just had a bad day, just like everyone else has. And believe me, I can tell you plenty of stories about feeling left out when I was growing up. This is just something that everyone goes through every now and then. You have good days and you have bad days."

Emma listens, but it feels like they are just words, words that mean nothing. She picks her head up and wipes her eyes on her long sleeve shirt. She feels just like a lost jigsaw puzzle piece; a piece that just can't find the one place where it fits. Maybe Tobias can find that lost piece. Maybe he knows where it fits.

Emma speaks in a soft feathery voice. "Mom, can I please walk to the woods? I promise that I'll be back by four."

Mom plants a kiss on the top of Emma's head. "Yes, you and Molly can go for a walk in the woods if you promise to come back feeling better." Mom grabs a breakfast bar and sticks it in Emma's hand. "And please, Emma, be sure that you eat this on the way."

"Thanks, Mom." Emma washes away her tears with both hands while holding onto the hope that she will feel better.

Chapter **13**
The Riddle

Emma doesn't bother changing her school clothes. She grabs her sweatshirt that hangs in the laundry room closet and hurries out the door. She is anxious to get to the woods. Emma almost feels as if something is calling her. Yet, she doesn't know what she will find.

Emma remembers that she didn't get her homework or her books when she went back to the classroom. It doesn't matter. Right now, nothing seems to matter at all.

Molly happily leads the way while prancing through the field. Puffy white clouds decorate a bright, blue sky. A slight breeze tickles the blades of grass. The warm sun showers down on Emma. Here she is, in the midst of it all, but not really. Emma feels like an observer, watching from somewhere high above, surrendering to whatever it is that is about to unfold.

The Riddle

Emma reaches the edge of the woods. She pauses and dusts the boulder with her right hand, soaking up and storing its warmth. She enters. The tree – where is the tree?

Emma keeps one eye on Molly, thinking that she might just lead her to the whereabouts of the treasure that she seeks. Molly happily bops from one tree to another. Apparently, she is completely clueless about the seriousness of this mission. It looks like she's not going to be much help.

Is that the tree? I remember that it had two low, large branches. They looked like two big arms; ready to scoop up whatever was below it.

Emma begins to trot to that particular tree in the distance. Getting closer, something catches her eyes. She recognizes the familiar stick that she had held in her hand. She walks to the tree and feels almost like hugging it. Yes, this is it! She falls to her knees even though she suspects that the ground remains damp, and she is still wearing her good school pants. What does it matter? Emma, so very softly, ruffles the new growth.

"Looking for something, Emma?"

Emma jumps up with a start. She quickly circles, searching for its source. She spots him. He is about seven yards away. Tobias, sitting on a knoll, is looking down at her.

"I – I was just looking for you."

Tobias rolls his big marble eyes, and a slight smile creeps across his face. "Ahh, Emma, that is music to my ears."

Emma slowly walks toward him, and a feeling of peace suddenly blankets her.

"Actually, I was expecting you, my dear."

Emma doesn't know what to say or do. Where does she begin? Should she say anything at all?

"So, you might say that, thus far, your day has not been so very pleasant."

Emma looks down as her right foot begins to scuff the ground. Her hands find her pockets. "That doesn't even come close to describing my day," she says with a shake of her head.

"Hmm, maybe you are feeling somewhat like a lost puzzle piece. Is that it, my dear?"

Emma's head springs up and her jaw drops down.

Tobias's eyes twinkle as he lets out a slight chuckle. "Let me ask you a question, dear Emma. What is your very favorite kind of ice cream?"

Emma is feeling rather puzzled. She wonders what is happening here, and how in the world they got on the topic of ice cream, of all things. "Well strawberry, I guess."

"For just a moment my dear, please imagine a world with strawberry ice cream – just strawberry. There is no chocolate ice cream. There is no vanilla. There is nothing at all but strawberry. Now tell me Emma, is strawberry still your favorite ice cream?"

Emma thinks. She searches for the answer. "Hmm. I – I guess that I really don't know."

"Really, and why is that?"

"Well, if there is nothing but strawberry then I don't know anything else. I have nothing to compare it to."

Tobias pushes one arm to the sky as if to show victory. He says in a booming voice, "Precisely my dear."

Emma contemplates what has just been said. Suddenly she feels light, so extremely light. "Hey, I think I get it! Yeah, I really get it. Maybe I really didn't have a bad day after all. Or maybe I needed to have the day that I had. I mean… I mean that if I never, ever had a bad day then I wouldn't really know what a good day was. They would all be just plain, ordinary days. Hmm, maybe even kinda boring." Emma smiles with pleasure.

Tobias nods, and he grins with satisfaction. In a whisper, he says –

"Riddle me diddle,
Life can be just so very simple.
The answer for you,
Is found in the lines of the haiku"

"Huh?" Emma is confused once again. "What the heck is a haiku?"

"You will tell me that on Saturday, my dear."

"How do I do that, and why do I have to wait until Saturday?"

"You will find the answer, dear Emma. Saturday will give you the time that you need. You know that you have much work to do. You have responsibilities to take care of."

Emma gives her forehead a hard rub. "Oh brother, now you sound just like my mother."

Tobias grins and gives Emma a quick wink. "Yes, my dear, but she may not be as old as I or as cute."

Chapter **14**

Haiku

There is one thing that Emma is sure of. She is a different person exiting the woods than she was on entering it. There is something different that she just can't pinpoint. Nor can she take the time or the energy to figure it out now. She has a task to complete. Emma needs to find out what a haiku is, and she needs to do this by Saturday.

I have to hurry and get home. Emma feels confused. "Haiku, that is such a weird word. I wonder what it means." Emma is afraid that she will forget this weird word. She keeps repeating it over and over again in her mind.

Haiku, haiku. Emma's steps are high and quick as she crosses the stretching field, up and down like the pistons on Dad's lawnmower that he so often tinkers with. Each high step pulls out that word - haiku.

With some luck, maybe Jake will help me find out what it means. Could it be some kind of book at the library?

Emma is getting more and more concerned. What if she can't find out what a haiku is? Should she still go back to the woods on Saturday?"

Emma is almost home. She can see Jake in the distance. He is playing catch, bouncing a ball against the back of the garage. "Haiku, haiku." Emma begins to run toward him with Molly in the lead.

Jake turns around as Molly joyfully pounces on him, wanting to play catch too. "Here she is. Gee Em, you sure look awfully sick!" He playfully tosses the ball to Em who makes no attempt to catch it. The ball blissfully bounces away.

"Jake, I saw Tobias." The words come pouring out. "He knew all about my day. He told me all this neat stuff about ice cream, but I have to find out what a haiku is, and I only have Saturday to do it."

Jake holds out one hand in stop fashion. "Hold on, Em. What the heck are you talking about?"

"A haiku. Jake, I have to write the word down, so I don't forget it. Will you help me?"

"Emma, I guess I can help you." Jake speaks slowly as he rubs his chin, "But I really don't know about this toad. Do ya think that he's an alien or somthin?"

"Jake, please! I can't forget this word."

"Alright, alright." They both head for the house.

Emma and Jake rush past Mom who is busy in the kitchen. "Hey Mom, I'm back from the woods. Jake and I are going upstairs. We're gonna check something out."

Mom turns around. With raised eyebrows, she watches them fly by. "Well, Emma, don't you sound refreshed!" She speaks up to be heard, "Glad you're feeling better."

Emma and Jake sprint up the stairs and head for Jake's room. He rifles through the pile on his desk and comes up with his tablet. "Found it. That word, haiku, sounds kind of familiar. I think that I heard it in school."

"I know that I've never heard of it before; sounds weird to me."

"I'll do Google search." Jake starts tapping letters. "Here's a definition. Ok, it's a Japanese poem. There is an English version. The poem has three lines with a total of 17 syllables.

Emma steps in closer to Jake and peers over his shoulder. "I know what syllables are."

Jake has his thinking face on. "Yeah, I remember now. The first line has five syllables, the second has seven, and the third one has five."

"Jake, that sounds kind of complicated. How am I supposed to remember all that?"

"There's more. I didn't know this."

Emma takes a step back. "Oh great!"

"It says that a haiku is a sort of meditation. It gives a feeling or an image."

"Meditation?" Emma steps up to Jake and gives his shoulder a jiggle. "I wonder what this is all about."

Jake turns and looks up with a serious face. "Emma, that is almost like a hug."

She ignores the comment. "You know Jake, Tobias seems to know all about me. He makes things clear in my head like with the ice cream. I wonder if he could be an angel or maybe a ghost. I tell ya, you've got to meet him!"

With raised eyebrows, Jake says, "Naw, I say that he's an alien. I bet on an alien toad." He puts his hand to his chin again and nods. "Yeah, I gotta meet this Tobias. He sounds like one cool dude.

Chapter **15**

Saturday

Drip, drip, drip. The hours and the days just drip by. Emma can't turn the faucet on any faster to make Saturday arrive any sooner.

She goes to school each day, and she works. She aces her Friday spelling test and even gets a ninety-six in math. Sometimes she sits with Chloe and other times she doesn't. She even forgets to tell her the news about Pete. Mary Rose's birthday party no longer seems important. Every day after school, Emma has a quick snack and then runs upstairs to get her homework done. She has responsibilities. She even helps around the house.

Thanks to Jake's help, Emma knows now what a haiku is. She has been practicing it over and over again in her head. She is anxious to show Tobias just how responsible she is.

Now Emma is nestled into bed while sleep fills her head. A purple quilted comforter tucks up to her chin. Emma rolls over to her belly while squishing the soft, plump pillow. Her left hand stretches out in search of her childhood companion, Barney the Brown Bear. Searching, searching, her hand can't find him. And with that, Emma pops up with a start.

It's Saturday! Today is Saturday!

Light pours into her windows. The time, it's eight-fourteen. Emma realizes that she didn't set her alarm. She flings her comforter to the floor, jumps out of bed, and heads for the stairs.

Mom and Dad are gathered over their morning coffee. Dad is the first to speak. "Here's my sunshine."

"Is Jake still sleeping?"

"Ryan's dad just picked him up for practice. You must have been sleeping pretty soundly. How about if I make you and Dad some waffles for breakfast?"

"Not for me, Mom. I think I'll take Molly for a walk to the woods." Emma drops two slices of bread into the toaster.

"This early?"

"I won't be gone long. Then I'll clean my room when we get back." Emma pours a glass of orange juice, takes her plate of toast, and heads for her room to get dressed. She can hear Mom and Dad speak in low voices.

"Scott, I don't know what the big attraction is in the woods all of a sudden."

"She's ok, Cathy. Molly will take care of her."

Hmm, Mom and Dad are talking about me.

Emma quickly washes. She is about to grab an old pair of jeans to wear but then thinks maybe not. Instead, she pulls out a nice pair of jeans and a pink striped hoodie. Emma steps back and looks at herself in the mirror. She gives herself a half-grin and a nod of her head.

"How silly am I being worried about what to wear for a toad!"

Emma hurries down the stairs. She grabs her denim jacket and a banana. "Let's go, Molly. See you guys in a bit."

Emma can feel the excitement in her body. She thought that Saturday would never come. The morning air is cool and crisp. There is a bit of a hazy mist.

As Emma begins to cross the field, her sneakers and pant legs soak up the moisture that wakens the earth to a new day. Emma can feel that this is not just an ordinary day. Emma picks her legs up high and sprints after Molly. She feels happy and playful. In no time at all, she reaches the woods.

For just a moment, Emma pauses at the boulder. For an unknown reason, she brushes it. Just a tad warm.

Emma walks confidently into the woods. The birds greet her with a cheerful good morning song. Her eyes skip about, looking for Tobias.

"Emma my dear, don't you look lovely as usual on this beautiful new day!"

Chapter **16**

Magic

Emma looks at Tobias, and for a moment she is speechless. Tobias gives her a quick wink.

Finally, she speaks. "I know what a haiku is."

"Indeed, you do! And dear Emma, I have a haiku just for you. Please follow me."

Tobias leads the way further into the woods. Emma feels rather silly following a hopping toad. Actually, she is quite surprised just how quickly he can hop.

"Yes, not so bad for an old toad. Right, Emma?"

Emma stops dead in her tracks. Hmm, he knows what I'm thinking again. She looks at Tobias, shakes her head, and then immediately continues walking as he leads the way. "Where are we going?"

"We are going to my palace, my dear."

A toad with a palace? Now Emma doesn't know what to think. They go just a bit further. Then they are unmistakably there.

They arrive at a bit of a clearing, enough so that the sunlight need not dance through the leaves of the trees. In fact, the sun appears as a spotlight. It radiates a brilliant golden light, warming every single thing that it touches.

The surrounding trees move softly and gracefully like that of the geisha. Emma doesn't feel a breeze at all. Every bit of green glistens as if the morning dew has painted each and every leaf with crystal.

"Wow!"

Emma senses life all about her. The birds sing as she has never heard them sing before. A tiny, white bunny with a fluffy powder puff tail scampers about. Emma is sure that it pauses and smiles at her. There are numerous insects humming a soft tune while beautiful butterflies of brilliant colors dance about.

Tobias turns and smiles at Emma. "My dear, you hear the soothing songs of the tiny insects. Let me assure you, they don't wish to have the song of the bird or the beauty of the butterfly." He points to the bunny. "See how my friend jumps with joy? He does not wish to have the flight of the bird." Tobias bends to stroke a stone that is sleeping by his feet. He looks up at Emma and smiles once again. "Even this precious stone finds peace in being a stone."

Emma stands silent as she weighs what has been said. Then something catches her eye.

Magic

Just about in the center of the clearing is a small, babbling brook. It seems to sprout magnificent bubbles that pop with all the colors in Emma's crayon box.

Emma looks at Tobias. She finally speaks. "Tobias, are you magic or what?"

Tobias turns his palms upward. He looks around with eyes that resemble twinkling stars. He speaks in almost a whisper. "Emma my dear, isn't it all just magic?"

For a moment, there is silence. Then Emma speaks. "I've been all through these woods, maybe a hundred times or more. I've never seen this place before."

In his slow, deep voice, Tobias replies, "Emma, do you think that you may have been looking through closed eyes?"

"Huh?"

With that, Tobias hops to the brook. He bows to the ground. He smooths an area of dark brown soil with his hand. And then, with one knobby finger, Tobias begins to painstaking write –

Living a king's life,
The secret of the toad is
Be a happy toad.

Slowly Tobias stands, turns, and looks at Emma. His eyes! His eyes are filled with the sun, and its warmth seems to envelope Emma. "You, my dear, have a palace hidden within you. You only need to find it."

Suddenly Tobias snaps his fingers, and Emma is caught up in a whirlwind of light. She squeezes her eyes shut tight and holds her breath. She feels as if she is tumbling, tumbling, tumbling about, in a sea of light.

Then the tumbling stops just as quickly as it started. Emma opens her eyes to find – all of it is gone.

Chapter **17**

The Mirror

Emma finds herself at the edge of the forest. Puzzled, she wonders how she got there? She walks up to the boulder. It has regained its warmth. She hops up onto it.

Suddenly, Molly appears. She paws at the boulder with a wildly wagging tail. She is wanting Emma's attention. Emma has lost all track of Molly. She briskly rubs her head and gives her ear an occasional gentle tug.

"Hey, girl. There you are. Where have you been, Molly? Maybe a better question is, where have I been?"

Emma isn't ready to leave just yet. She recalls everything that's happened. It reels fast forward in her mind.

How is it that she and Jake have been to these woods so many times, and they never stumbled on that magical place before? But then again, Tobias said that it is all magic. Will she ever be able to find that very same spot in the woods again?

Just who is Tobias? How does he know so much about her? Why did he take her to his palace? Where else might he lead her?

The sights and the sounds that Emma just experienced – she wants to hold them captive forever. Does she share these moments with anyone? With Jake? Would anyone believe her? Emma is filled with so many questions.

Then she remembers – the haiku. Yes, it's all about the haiku. With the tip of her finger, Emma begins to pen out the words on the face of the boulder. Emma knows that she cannot let these words escape.

> Living a king's life,
> The secret of the toad is
> Be a happy toad.

Emma realizes that just as she has etched out this haiku on the boulder, it is also etched into her heart. Yes, she may have questions, but she has discovered something very important about herself, as well. With that, Emma looks across the field. The mist has lifted. She slips off the rock. She is ready to go home.

Emma begins to cross the field. She finds herself twirling, as if on a magnificent carousel, in the middle of nowhere. A rainbow of colors splashes all about her. The sunlight whirls with her, like it's her dancing partner. Soft music lifts her up and settles her down, as she enjoys the carousel ride home.

In the distance, Emma sees her home. It is as if she is experiencing the scene frame by frame, all in slow motion. Emma can see clothes hanging from the line. She thinks how the different clothes – jeans, Dad's dress shirts, Jake's baseball uniform, they can almost tell her family story.

Dad is kneeling in the driveway. He is tinkering with the lawnmower once again, getting it ready to cut the grass.

Molly just about plows Mom over with a kiss on the cheek, as Mom is about to lift a pile of weeds to the wheelbarrow. With her hard work, their yard will soon explode with flowers.

Tobias is right. It is all magical.

"Hey Mom, we're back."

"That's just what Molly said. Did you have a nice walk?"

"It was a great walk, Mom. I think I'll go and clean my room."

Emma kicks off wet sneaks and tugs off wet socks. She deposits her jacket on the top of the dryer. She takes two stairs at a time.

Entering her room, Emma spots a furry, brown paw poking from beneath the purple comforter that had found its way to the floor. She stoops down to retrieve it. "There you are, Barney. What are you doing on the floor? I was looking for you, silly bear."

Emma steps in front of Gram's mirror. She peers intently. A smile suddenly springs across her face.

Emma sees a reflection. It is the reflection of a beautiful princess, holding a stuffed brown bear in the crook of her arm.

Emma then realizes that this princess has arrived – on the tail of a comet!

The Mirror